A Note to Parents

Reading books aloud and playing word games are two valuable ways parents can help their children learn to read. The easy-to-read stories in the **My First Hello Reader! With Flash Cards** series are designed to be enjoyed together. Six activity pages and 16 flash cards in each book help reinforce phonics, sight vocabulary, reading comprehension, and facility with language. Here are some ideas to develop your youngster's reading skills:

Reading With Your Child
- Read the story aloud to your child and look at the colorful illustrations together. Talk about the characters, setting, action, and descriptions. Help your child link the story to events in his or her own life.
- Read parts of the story and invite your child to fill in the missing parts. At first, pause to let your child "read" important last words in a line. Gradually, let your child supply more and more words or phrases. Then take turns reading every other line until your child can read the book independently.

Enjoying the Activity Pages
- Treat each activity as a game to be played for fun. Allow plenty of time to play.
- Read the introductory information aloud and make sure your child understands the directions.

Using the Flash Cards
- Read the words aloud with your child. Talk about the letters and sounds and meanings.
- Match the words on the flash cards with the words in the story.
- Help your child find words that begin with the same letter and sound, words that rhyme, and words with the same ending sound.
- Challenge your child to put flash cards together to make sentences from the story and create new sentences.

Above all else, make reading time together a fun time. Show your child that reading is a pleasant and meaningful activity. Be generous with your praise and know that, as your child's first and most important teacher, you are contributing immensely to his or her command of the printed word.

—Tina Thoburn, Ed.D.
Educational Consultant

Library of Congress Cataloging-in-Publication Data

Jensen, Patricia.
   A funny man / by Patricia Jensen ; illustrated by Wayne Becker.
      p.   cm.
   Summary: A funny man with a funny smile, funny car, and funny crocodile likes to do things just a little bit differently.
   ISBN 0-590-46193-1
   [1. Individuality—Fiction. 2. Stories in rhyme.] I. Becker, Wayne, ill. II. Title.
PZ8.3.J424Fu   1993
[E]—dc20   92-36007
                                                                CIP
                                                                 AC

25 24 23 22 21 20 19 18 17   8/9

Printed in the U.S.A.   24
First Scholastic printing, October 1993

A FUNNY MAN

by Patricia Jensen
Illustrated by Wayne Becker

My First Hello Reader!
With Flash Cards

SCHOLASTIC INC.

New York   Toronto   London   Auckland   Sydney

Cartwheel
·B·O·O·K·S· ®

There was a funny man.

He had a funny smile.

He had a funny car

and a funny crocodile.

He had a funny hat

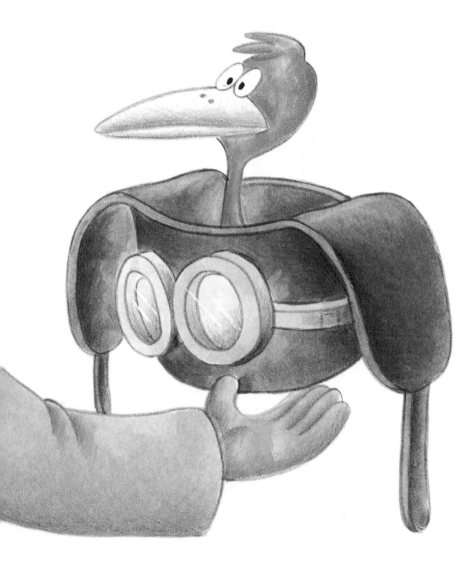

upon his funny head.

there	had
a	funny
man	he
was	smile

was  normal

in sort

of way

head funny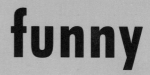

then	got
he	bed
dream	about
day	everything

his	and
crocodile	hat
upon	a
car	dinner

He had a funny dinner.

Then he got in bed.

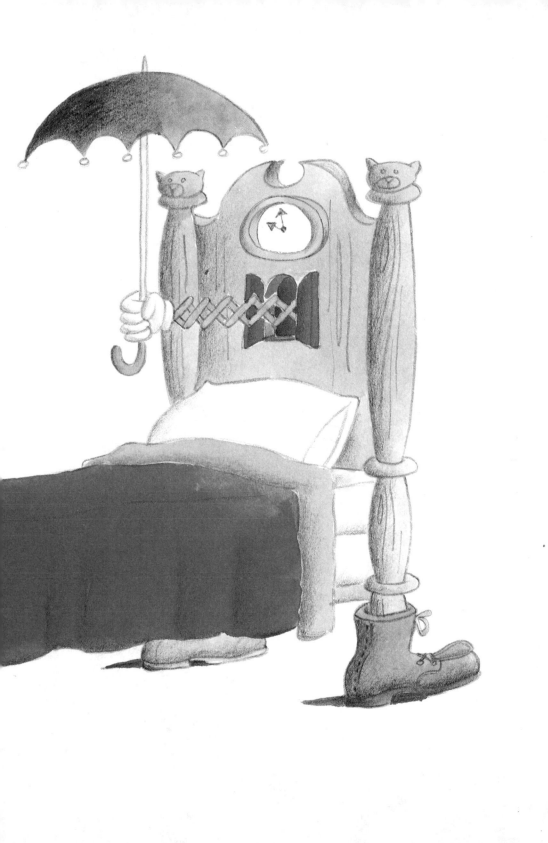

He had a funny dream

about his funny day.

And everything was normal—
in a funny sort of way.

All in a Word

Every time you see the word *funny* in this story, use the word *little* instead. How does this change the story?

Now try the word *happy*.

Can you think of any other words that you could use instead of *funny* to change the meaning of this story?

Picture Match

Point to the picture that matches each word.

man

crocodile

hat

car

Something's Funny Here

See how many things you can find that are wrong with this picture.

In the Beginning

Look at the word *funny*. If you take away the **f** and put in a **b**, you have the word *bunny*. What word do you have if you take away the **f** and put in an **s**?

Can you make new words by changing the first letters of these words, too?

 man

 hat

 day

At the End

What happens if you take away the **r** at the end of the word *car* and put in a different letter? Try an **n**. What word do you have now? Try a **p** and then a **t**.

Can you make new words by changing the last letters of these words, too?

man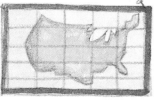

had

his

Answers

(In the Beginning)

sunny

man—*can*

hat—*bat*

day—*hay*

(At the End)

can cap cat

man—*map*

had—*hat*

his—*hit*